The Little Girl with the Plow

By Christina Chislom
Illustrations by Pia Neal

J Merrill Publishing, Inc.
434 Hillpine Drive
Columbus, OH 43207
www.JMerrill.pub

ISBN-13: 978-1-954414-33-4 (Paperback)
ISBN-13: 978-1-954414-32-7 (eBook)

Book Title: The Little Girl with the Plow!
Author: Christina Chislom
Illustration: Pia Neal

Any references to historical events, real people, or real places are used fictitiously. Names, characters, and places are products of the author's imagination.

There was a little girl named Lee. She lived in a beautiful place called Harvest Town, along with her mother, Mrs. Jeanette, the best cook in town. Everyone loved to smell her tasty treats cooking every day.

Her father, Mr. Rocky, was the town's Plowman.

She has three brothers. Nick, the oldest, was strong and smart, but he was always jealous of his sister. Ricky, the middle brother, was always ready to help, but he was sometimes afraid. Then there's her youngest brother, William. He was the cutest one. And he was always wondering if he was good enough.

Oh yeah, and Jack, he was the family dog. He loved to bark. They loved their Harvest Town, and the town loved them.

Harvest Town was a beautiful place with lots of land, lots of trees, and happy people. Harvest Town was known for its fruits and vegetables.

Everyone grew their own food, and Mr. Rocky was very important to Harvest Town because he was the Plow Man.

After the cold winters, Mr. Rocky would get his plow ready to prepare the soil so the people could plant and get ready for the spring and summer harvest.

Everyone counted on him. He was the best plowman in town. Mr. Rocky loved to plow, and he taught all of his children how to plow just like he did. He hoped his children would love to plow and take over the family business one day and continue to keep Harvest Town beautiful.

Lee loved to ride along with her father on his plow machine. She loved to learn and loved to see the fields grow. She was really good at it, just like her dad, even though she was a little girl.

Lee's brothers learned how to plow, too. But Nick was always jealous of her, Ricky was always afraid of what his friends would say, and William always thought he was too short to help. So when it was time for Mr. Rocky to plow, Lee was the first one ready to go.

One winter, Mr. Rocky became very sick and was too weak to plow for the spring-summer harvest, and it was time for the soil to be turned over and new seeds to be planted.

The townspeople were all sad because they knew Mr. Rocky was sick and needed someone to plow. So the people of the town called a meeting to see how they could get ready for harvest time.

WHO WILL PLOW?

The townspeople brainstormed for hours, and their shouting got louder and louder until the Harvest Town Police had to come to see what all the fuss was about.

Then, just as the police were going to send everyone there home with no solution, a small hand went up, and a loud voice of a little girl shouted I know how to plow.

Everyone there turned and looked at Lee.

Some people began to laugh; some walked away saying, "no little girl can handle this job."

But the mayor of the town said to give the little girl a chance, she is the plow man's daughter, maybe she can handle the plow.

So, excited and a little nervous, Lee ran all the way home to tell her father the good news.

So Lee went to her oldest brother Nick, and asked will you help me plow for Harvest time? He seemed angry and said, "Why would they ask you and not me. You're a little girl, and I learned to plow first. No, I will not help you plow."

This made Lee very sad. Still, she asked her other brothers to join the team. She asked Ricky her, middle brother, will he plow? He said, "I'm afraid of what happens if we can't finish." But, Lee said, "You are strong and brave, and as long as we work together, we will finish the job." So Ricky got the courage to come along.

Together they went to ask William, their youngest brother, will you help us plow? He said, "I'm too short. I can barely reach the seat. There is no way I can plow." Lee said, "We will boost you up ourselves. You can do it. Be confident and Believe in yourself. You're not too short; it's just right for you!" William gained his confidence and said, "Yes, as long as we are together, I will plow."

Mr. Rocky saw his children getting ready for the big task ahead, and he was very proud. Just one person was missing, he thought, my oldest son, Nick.

So Mr. Rocky went out to talk to Nick and said, "You are my oldest son. I taught you everything I know, and there is no reason for you to be jealous. Parents love all their children, and we believe in you. Your brothers and sister need you. This town needs you. Will you go and plow?"

Nick thought long and hard. Then, finally, he looked out the window to his town and remembered his father's words, "We need you."

Nick could not leave his brothers and sister to plow alone. So he ran down to the place where the plowing would begin.

Ricky, who was once afraid, was on his machine, ready to plow. Their dog Jack came along and gave William a boost up to his seat. He sat down on his machine and got ready to plow, Jack by his side.

Lee was ready to get on her machine when she heard the sound of another plow machine coming down the field. She looked up she saw her brother Nick riding down the field. She was so excited!

All her brothers cheered as they looked each other in the eyes, put on their sunglasses, gave each other a nod of the head, and together they began to Plow.

Lee was leading the way. They plowed all day until they turned over all the soil in Harvest Town.

The planters came behind them and planted their seeds in the ground. The sun shined, the rains came, the harvest grew. It was the best harvest the town ever had.

Lee and her family were so happy they began to celebrate together for a job well done. Mrs. Jeanette gathered the best fruits and vegetables and began to prepare a great harvest supper.

When the family sat down at the table, Mr.Rocky asked his oldest son, Nick, to bless the food. Nick said these words, "God, we thank you for our food, for our family, especially my little sister, Lee, our little girl with the plow, and we thank you for harvest time!" They all cheered right at the table and ate the best supper ever.

THE END

Word Search

```
S I S T E R T O J T
P B L H D G E S E H
L R L A A I A H A E
O A I R D R M O L F
W V T V F L W R O A
M E T E E O O T U M
O U L S A V R P S I
M C E T R E K B O L
N B R O T H E R M Y
P C T O W N D O G A
```

Teamwork	Harvest	Brother	Family
Sister	Fear	Plow	Brave
Love	Town	Short	Jealous
Dog	Little	Girl	Dad
The	Mom		

Baby Lee

By, J.Jamar Chrisp

Can you draw in and color...
The Sun,
Clouds,
A Tree,
and Jack the Dog?

Mr. Rocky
By, J.Jamar Chrisp

About the Author...

Christina Chislom has worked with children since she was a little girl herself! From directing The "Rosebud" choir at her childhood church to working at daycares and coordinating her first Vacation Bible School! She enjoys working with children of all ages and has a love for making them smile!

At the age of 41, she still has fun with coloring and activity books! That is actually the reason she decided to write this book.

Christina's father's life inspired her to write this book, the late William Lee (Charlene) Chislom. Christina's dad always taught her to be strong, independent, and courageous. She hopes every child who reads this book will be empowered to do big things.

The book is about girl power, sibling love, overcoming insecurities, and the importance of family.

Christina was influenced by Mother Naomi Loggins (P.C.COGIC) and Kathy Houser-McGee (5th & 6th grade-teacher) as a young lady. Throughout her teenage years, her influencers were Natalie Janel Koch (youth pastor) and Dawn Axel (auntie and lover of children). As an adult, she has been influenced by Apostle Wayman Thomas, who taught me how to "Plow" in the spirit! (Apostolic Father). She is thankful for the many mentors she's had so far and those yet to come!

Christina holds a Pastoral Degree from Valor Bible College (Columbus, Ohio - Dr. Rod Parsley).
She serves faithfully in her local church Rebirth Columbus under the encouragement, excellence, and love of Apostle Darren (Sonya) Thomas.

About the Illustrator...

Pia Josephine Neal is a 15-year-old sophomore at Grove City High School, where she participates in the Marching Band and Honors Choir.

Pia has always enjoyed the arts and has a big group of supporters! Pia's family and friends have cheered her on, whether it's singing on stage, creating new art, and, most importantly, trying new things!

Pia has a true love and appreciation for learning and spends a lot of time exploring history and how to learn from it. Pia was incredibly honored to partner with Christina with "The Little Girl with the Plow."

This story meant the world to Pia. She believes everyone can benefit from reading about a little girl who powers through against the odds and brings her family and an entire town together.

CPSIA information can be obtained
at www.ICGtesting.com
Printed in the USA
BVRC101316281221
625052BV00003B/151